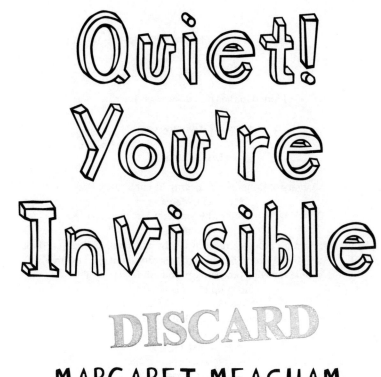

Quiet! You're Invisible

MARGARET MEACHAM

HOLIDAY HOUSE / New York

First Edition

Library of Congress Cataloging-in-Publication Data
Meacham, Margaret.
Quiet! You're invisible / by Margaret Meacham.—1st ed.
p. cm.
Summary: With his mother expecting a baby and a bully living next door,
fifth grader Hoby Hobson has enough to worry about even before Zirc,
a time-traveling boy who can sometimes be invisible,
shows up in his backyard.
ISBN 0-8234-1651-8 (hardcover)
[1. Time travel—Fiction. 2. Bullies—Fiction.] I. Title.

PZ7.M47886 Qu 2001
[Fic]—dc21
2001016719

For John,
still funny after all these years.
Amor in Aeternum

chapter one

Hoby Hobson was halfway underneath his bed, looking for his left sneaker, when Taz barked. Hoby rolled out from under the bed and sat up, bumping his head on the way. Taz barked again and again. Hoby's stomach knotted up. His hands shook. He took a deep breath. Get a grip, he told himself. It's just Taz.

A week ago the sound of Taz barking would not have fazed him. A week ago he had been a normal kid—well, maybe not totally normal, but not the shivering, quivering mass of fear he was today. A week ago he had made the biggest mistake of his life. Now he was doomed to spend the rest of it hiding from his neighbor Hammerhead Jones.

Why had he done it? Hoby had asked himself that question at least a hundred times in the past week.

He thought back to the day it had happened. He had been mad at Hammerhead, and for good reason. Hammerhead was an overgrown bully. The list of his victims was endless. Evan Harper was stuffed into a trash can after refusing to give Hammerhead the chocolate chip cookies Evan had gotten in his lunch. Cecil Spaygo was used as a toilet plunger (headfirst) because he refused to call Hammerhead "sir." No fifth grader was safe when Hammerhead was around. But that day, the day it had happened, Hammerhead had done something that made Hoby even madder than usual.

It happened in middle-school assembly. Some dancers had come in to give a performance, and then they took questions from the kids. Carrie Bateman raised her hand and said she was thinking about becoming a dancer, and Hammerhead laughed. The way Carrie looked when Hammerhead laughed at her made Hoby mad—really, really mad. True, Carrie was kind of a klutz. She could hardly walk down the hall without tripping and spilling her books everywhere. Maybe she wouldn't have made the greatest dancer in the world, but still, in Hoby's opinion, people had a right to their dreams, and they shouldn't be laughed at because of them.

Walking past the Joneses' house on his way home that day, Hoby remembered the black Magic Marker in his pocket. He had borrowed it from Patience during art and had forgotten to give it back. The Joneses' white fence called to him the way a clean new canvas calls to an artist. The Magic Marker was out of his pocket, and before he knew what he was doing, he had drawn a portrait of Hammerhead. The portrait was not a flattering one, though Hoby felt it was some of the best artwork he'd ever done. He had somehow managed to capture the demented look in Hammerhead's bulging eyes. It was that look, and the way his eyes protruded from his round, fat face, that had earned Hammerhead his nickname. His real name was Harold Jones, but behind his back everyone called him Hammerhead. Below the picture Hoby had written "Beware of Shark." He was admiring his finished work when a shadow fell across the fence. Hoby didn't dare look behind him, but he knew who it was. Dread crept from his toes to the pit of his stomach.

"What do you think you're doing?" Hammerhead snarled. For a minute Hoby just stood there. Then something happened to him. It was as if he had been sleepwalking, and all of a sudden he woke up and realized that he was standing here in plain sight, drawing graffiti on Hammerhead Jones's fence. What *did* he think he was doing? Such a good question. An excellent question. Unfortunately, it was a question that Hoby couldn't answer.

"I asked you a question," Hammerhead growled. Hoby could feel his mouth moving, but no sound was coming out. Apparently he had forgotten how to talk. He thought about running, but he had forgotten how to walk.

Then Hoby was flying. He flew over the hedge and landed in a crumpled heap in his own backyard. Hammerhead had lofted him like a paper airplane. Hammerhead started to come after him again, but luckily Mrs. Jones drove up and called him. Hammerhead stopped, but he said, "I'll take care of you later. Would you rather be pounded into mashed potatoes or sliced into french fries? Sautéed or filleted?" Mrs. Jones was a cook, so Hammerhead tended to use a lot of food metaphors.

"I—I'll think about it and let you know," Hoby replied.

"You do that," Hammerhead said.

Now Hoby lived in fear, expecting Hammerhead to appear at any moment, never knowing when he might strike. It was awful. Hammerhead was in seventh grade, two grades ahead of Hoby. He was huge, at least a foot taller and forty pounds heavier than Hoby. And he was meaner than a hungry shark.

Why had he done it? Hoby asked himself again and again. He had never even written on the bathroom walls at school. He just wasn't the type who went around drawing graffiti. Why had he suddenly decided to do it? And on the Joneses' fence, of all places.

"Hoby, go out and see what Taz is barking at, will you?" his mother called to him from her bedroom.

"I can see him from here, Mom. It's nothing. Probably the Bidwells' cat."

Hoby's mother laughed. "Don't be silly, Hoby, Taz is terrified of the Bidwells' cat. He'd be begging to come in the house if she were out there. It must be something else. Please go and see."

Hoby stepped out the back door and peered around the yard. He dropped to the ground. Nothing happened. Taz trotted over to him and licked his face. Taz was an English bulldog. He had short little legs that looked like they would barely support his plump body and a big round wrinkly face with a toothy grin and soft brown eyes.

"Quiet, boy. No more barking," Hoby whispered. Then the hammock moved. There was something in it. Hoby's heart was pounding so hard he thought he might faint. Was it Hammerhead, lying in wait for him?

He crawled toward the hammock, ready to make a fast retreat if he needed to. Taz crept, too, wrinkling up his forehead and making a low growling sound, trying to seem fierce. The hammock moved again.

"Hoby? Are you all right?" his mother called from the upstairs window.

"I'm fine, Mom," Hoby called.

Since Hoby's mother was eight-and-a-half months pregnant, Hoby had to be very careful not to upset her. He knew it was easy to upset pregnant people because of what his friend Barney had told him. Barney had three younger brothers and a younger sister, so he was practically an expert on having babies. Once Barney's mom had started crying just because Barney had eaten all the rocky road ice cream. "I didn't know she even liked rocky road," Barney had said.

"If you're all right, why are you crawling across the yard?" Hoby's mom asked.

"Why am I crawling? Because, um, my legs are kind of tired today and, I don't know, I just sort of dropped to the ground."

"Hoby, for heaven's sake. Come in and finish your breakfast or you'll be late for school again," his mom said, shutting the window.

Hoby started to get up when all of a sudden a pair of legs appeared right in front of him.

"Aaahhh!" Hoby screamed, and dropped to his stomach again, covering his head with his hands. Taz buried his face under Hoby's arm.

"Oh, hey, I'm sorry. I didn't mean to scare you," said a voice.

Hoby looked up. A boy was standing in front of him. It was not Hammerhead. Slowly Hoby stood up. The boy looked about his own age. He was a little smaller than Hoby and he wore an army green jumpsuit with COMETS printed across the front. He had reddish brown hair and a friendly face.

"Wh-where did you come from?" Hoby asked. "You weren't here a minute ago."

"I was here," the boy said. "You just didn't see me."

"Oh," Hoby said. "Um, are you lost or something?"

"Well, sort of," the boy said.

"Do you live around here?" Hoby asked.

"Um, not exactly," the boy said.

"*Hobeee!*" Hoby's mother called from the house.

Hoby glanced up at the window. "Coming, Mom." He turned back to the boy. "Well, I gotta—hey!" The boy was gone.

Hoby looked at Taz. Taz looked at Hoby.

Hoby shivered. "There's something really weird going on around here, Tazzy."

chapter two

Inside, Hoby took a deep breath, trying to calm himself. He wasn't hungry, but he poured himself a bowl of cereal and sat down to eat it. His mom came into the kitchen. Hoby stared at her. Her stomach had gotten bigger overnight. She was huge, well, at least her stomach was. It made Hoby nervous just to look at her.

"Oh, I love this song," his mom said, turning up the radio. "Your father and I used to dance to this in college." To Hoby's horror, she began dancing at the sink as she washed up the breakfast dishes.

"Mom, Mom! What are you doing?" Hoby yelled.

"I'm washing the dishes, Hoby."

"But you're dancing. You can't dance in your condition, Mom, it's—it's not safe."

His mother laughed. "Oh, Hoby. Just because I'm pregnant doesn't mean I'm sick. I can still dance if I want." She bounced and swayed, singing into the dish scrubber as if it were a microphone.

"I gotta go. See you later, Mom." Hoby grabbed his backpack and hurried out of the house.

When he saw Barney at lunch, Hoby said, "Did your mother ever dance when she was pregnant?"

"No, she didn't dance. But she did yoga. That's worse."

After school, Hoby was turning into his own driveway when someone yanked his collar back. He knew who it was before he looked over his shoulder and saw Hammerhead's fat face peering down at him the way a toad peers at a fly.

"I've been waiting for you," Hammerhead said.

"Y-you have?" Hoby said. This was not good news.

"I want to ask you something. And if you give me the right answer, I might let you go."

"Wh-what if I give the wrong answer?" Hoby asked.

Hammerhead gave him a sickening grin. "Do you really want to know?"

"M-maybe not."

"I'm looking for a skinny kid in a green jump-suit. He was snooping around my yard when I got home from school a few minutes ago. But now he's gone. You know anything about him?"

It was the kid who'd been in Hoby's yard that morning, he was sure of it. He was about to tell Hammerhead what he knew about him when something stopped him. He hated the thought of Hammerhead pounding the kid to bits. Hoby realized he should be grateful that Hammerhead wanted to pound this new kid instead of him, but he wasn't. Then he had a brilliant idea. He said, "I think I might know who you mean."

"Yeah? Well, help me find him. I don't like people snooping around my yard."

"I wouldn't mess with that kid if I were you, Harold."

"Oh yeah? Why not?"

"I think his dad is the new police chief," Hoby said.

The grip on Hoby's collar tightened. Hammerhead stared down at him, one eye scrunched shut, the other huge and red-rimmed, floating over him. Hoby could see his own reflection in it, small and scared.

"You're sure about this?" Hammerhead asked.

"Well, I'm pretty sure. I mean, that's what I heard," Hoby said.

Hammerhead continued to peer down at him. What was going to happen? Would they stay like this forever? Then, from out of nowhere, a half-rotten apple sailed through the air and landed with a satisfying splat on Hammerhead's left ear.

"Hey," he bellowed, releasing Hoby in his surprise.

Hoby didn't hang around to find out where the apple had come from. He raced for his house and was inside before Hammerhead had wiped the rotten goop from his hair.

chapter three

Hoby sat at his desk staring at his homework. He had survived another day. He was not mashed potatoes or french fries. He had not been sautéed or filleted. But what about tomorrow? How long could he go on like this? Hammerhead was ruining his life. And nobody understood. Even the twins, Patrick and Patience, his best friends, were annoyed with him. He had tried to explain to them about Hammerhead, but they really didn't understand.

"You worry too much," Patrick told him. "Hammerhead's just a bully. You've got to stand up to him."

"Yeah, right," Hoby said. But he knew Patrick was right. He didn't want to be a wimp. Especially now that he was about to be a big brother. Nobody wanted a wimp for a big brother.

Hoby had dreamed of standing up to Hammerhead. He slid out of his desk chair and lay on his back on the floor. Taz came over and licked his face. "You'd take on Jaws while I clobbered Hammerhead, wouldn't you, boy?" Jaws was Hammerhead's huge Great Dane who was chained to the Joneses' porch. He growled at everyone who passed. Taz panted. When Taz panted it sounded as though he was saying, "Yeah a yeah a yeah." Hoby loved that about him. Taz always agreed with him, no matter what Hoby said.

"Yeah. We'll clobber 'em, won't we, fella?"

"Yeah a yeah a yeah," said Taz.

Hoby was about to get back to his homework when he thought he heard someone in his bathroom. His dad was working late tonight. It could only be his mother.

"Mom?" he called.

The shower was running. Why would his mom be taking a shower in Hoby's bathroom instead of her own? And why now? She always took her shower in the morning.

He knocked on the bathroom door. "Mom?" The shower stopped, but there was no answer. He knocked again. Still no answer. He opened the door a bit. "Mom, are you in here?"

He opened the door wider. The tub was wet, and the bathroom was all steamy. But empty.

Great, now he was imagining things. Hammerhead really was getting to him.

Hoby ran downstairs and found his mom in her office. She worked at a graphic design firm, but she had an office at home, too. Lately, because of the baby, she did a lot of her work at home. She was standing at the fax machine, wearing a football helmet. The rest of her was dressed normally in one of his dad's big sweatshirts and the special jeans that fit over the baby. But the football helmet worried Hoby. The weird behavior that Barney had warned him about was beginning. First dancing, now football.

"Um, Mom?"

"What is it, Hoby?" she asked.

"Nothing, Mom. I was just wondering if you were in the shower."

"Do I look like I'm in the shower, Hoby?" she asked.

"No, but . . . "

"If I'm standing here in my office, how could I be in the shower?"

"Well, see, that's just what I was wondering."

She smiled and ruffled his hair. "Hoby, sometimes you mystify me."

"Um, Mom?"

"Yes, Hoby?"

"You're wearing a football helmet."

"Yes, I am," she said, tearing off her fax and reading it.

"So are you going to be playing football then?" Hoby asked.

"I hadn't planned on it," his mother said.

"That's good, because I really don't think it's a good idea," Hoby told her.

"No. I've never liked football," she said.

"So, the helmet is, like, a fashion statement?" Hoby asked.

"No, actually, I was in the basement. It's filthy down there, full of cobwebs and things. Stuff was dropping on me. I put the helmet on to protect my hair and then I heard the fax go off," she explained. "Now, are we clear on the shower issue, Hoby?"

"Yes, Mom."

"Okay, then. Back to your homework." His mom put the fax away and left her office. "I'm going back down to the basement, Hoby. I'm trying to find the boxes of baby clothes and toys left from when you were a baby."

"Okay, Mom."

Back upstairs, Hoby stopped outside his bathroom door. Someone was in there. Whoever it was was whistling. Hoby flung open the door. The boy who'd been in his yard that morning was standing in front of the mirror, naked except for the towel wrapped around his waist. He was combing his hair, but when he saw Hoby he dropped the comb and screamed. Hoby screamed, too, and behind him Taz let out a startled little growl.

Hoby and the boy stared at each other. Hoby wondered if he should call his mother, but then he remembered the speech his father had given him a few weeks ago. "Your mother will be working at home more often now," he had said. "This means she needs peace and quiet to get her work done. Try not to interrupt her. Remember the three F's: flood, fire, and fatal illness. If it's not one of the three F's, use your ingenuity and handle it yourself." Hoby didn't see how finding a strange boy in his bathroom qualified as one of the three F's, and besides, his mom was down in the basement. He decided not to call her.

The boy was fussing with a band on his wrist. "This flibbin' dematerializer. It must be razzed up again." He looked at Hoby and sighed. His body seemed to deflate and he looked lost, almost as if he might start to cry. Hoby forgot to be afraid and felt sorry for him.

"I guess you're wondering what I'm doing here, huh?" the boy said.

"Well, yeah," Hoby said.

"See, the thing is, you're not supposed to be able to see me. I should be invisible, but my dematerializer's not working right." He tapped on the band and all of a sudden—zap—the boy vanished!

"There we go. That's more like it," the boy's voice said.

Wait a minute, Hoby thought. Was this really happening? The boy was there, and then he was gone. Poof. It was a dream. It had to be.

There was another zap and the boy was back. "I really should get this flibbin' thing looked at," he said, holding the band to his ear and shaking his wrist. He looked at Hoby again. "The thing is, I really need to talk to you, but I wanted to take a shower first. See, I came here right from flizball practice, and then sleeping in your hammock last night didn't help. By the way, my name is Zircus. Zircus Orflandu. Most people call me Zirc."

chapter four

Hoby backed out of the bathroom and ran into his own room across the hall. "Don't worry, Taz, it's just a dream."

Zirc followed him, still wearing only a towel, but carrying his green jumpsuit. As he came into Hoby's room, he tripped and knocked over a lamp on the desk.

"I'm sorry. I'm such a yadzuu."

"A what?" Hoby asked.

"A yadzuu. Like, I'm always knocking things over."

"Oh. A klutz. Well, don't worry about it," Hoby said, calmly picking up the lamp. "These things happen in dreams."

"You think this is a dream? Huh, I wish it was. So, what did you say your name was?" Zirc asked.

Hoby sat down on his bed. Taz sat down and leaned against Hoby's legs, glaring at the boy and trying his best to look fierce.

"I'm Hoby Hobson. And this is Taz."

"Well, Hoby, I guess you're wondering why I was sleeping in your hammock and taking a shower in your bathroom," Zirc said.

"Um, sort of." Hoby didn't want to be rude, but it was strange. "I mean, if I want to take a shower, I usually do it at my own house," he told Zirc.

"Yeah, course you do. So would I. If I could."

"You don't have a shower?" Hoby asked.

"No, it's not that. It's worse than that."

"You don't have a house?"

"I do, but my house is a thousand years from here."

"You mean a thousand miles," Hoby said.

"No." Zirc frowned. "I wish that was it, but see, I got here in my father's new space cruiser, which has a time module. I didn't mean to go anywhere. I was just sitting in it, wishing I were old enough to cruise, you know? Anyway, all I meant to do was to turn the soundport on to listen to some music, but I must have pushed the wrong button because all of a sudden I was zooming through time. I ended up exactly a thousand years from home. The bad thing is, the battery on the time module is weak, and it will take a few days for it to charge. And if I don't get back soon, I'm going to be in big trouble."

Hoby stared at the boy. There he was, standing in the middle of the room, wearing a towel, and talking about time modules and space cruisers. This is some dream, Hoby thought.

"Your father's space cruiser? Is that like an airplane?" Hoby asked.

"A space cruiser is, well, why don't you come and see it for yourself? It's docked right out there in the woods behind your house. I guess that's where our cruiser deck is in my time."

"You're telling me you came here from the next millennium. That you actually traveled through time?"

"Sure. We do it all the time. Usually we stay invisible, though. And kids aren't allowed to go by themselves. You have to be eighteen to time travel alone. That's one reason why I'll be in big trouble if I don't get home soon."

"Wow. Can we go see the space cruiser now?" Hoby figured it was just a dream, after all. But then again Zirc seemed very real, not at all dreamlike.

"Sure," Zirc said. "Just let me make myself invisible. But wait, before I do, do you think you could lend me some pants and a shirt? This jumpsuit is kind of greeb."

"Sure." Hoby went to his bureau, pulled out a T-shirt and a pair of jeans, and handed them to Zirc. "What's greeb?" he asked.

"Greeb is, um, it means it really badly needs to be washed," Zirc explained. "See, I had just gotten home from flizball practice. I was on my way to shower and change, but then I saw the new space cruiser on the deck, and I thought it wouldn't hurt anything if I just sat in it for a minute."

Hoby nodded. Sometimes he liked to sit in his dad's car, pretending he could drive, imagining the day when he'd have his own car.

"What's flizball?" he asked.

"Flizball? You don't have it yet? Veeb, that's too bad. Flizball is zall."

"Zall? Is that good?" Hoby asked.

"The best," Zirc told him.

"I play baseball and soccer. I like basketball, too, but I'm not tall enough to make the team."

Zirc nodded, pulling on Hoby's T-shirt. "I remember studying about some of those old sports when we did our unit on the twenty-first century. Flizball is kind of a combination of soccer and basketball, except you play it on a special court that's gravity controlled to make you almost weightless. You can zoom all over, up in the air and everything."

"Do you need anything else?" Hoby asked politely as Zirc finished dressing.

"There is one other thing," Zirc said. "And it's really important." He picked up the green jumpsuit, reached into the pocket, and pulled out a shiny silver square about the size of a small calculator. "This is the battery for the time module. It needs to be kept at subfreezing temperatures in order for it to recharge. Do you think we could put it in your tempulator?"

"We don't have a tempulator. But we have a freezer. I could put it in there." The freezer was pretty messy, full of stuff that had been in there for months. He could put it in the back and no one would ever notice.

"Great! You're zall, Hoby."

Hoby took the battery. "Come on. Let's put it in the freezer and then we can go look at your space cruiser."

There was a zap and Zirc disappeared. "I'd better stay invisible. I don't want your parents to see me. I don't want anyone else to know about me. It could really razz things up. Time travelers aren't supposed to be seen."

"Right," Hoby said. He definitely did not want his parents to see Zirc. "This way."

Downstairs in the kitchen, Hoby opened the freezer and put the battery in the very back underneath a box of frozen waffles.

"No ice cream now, Hoby," his mom said as she came into the kitchen and saw Hoby looking into the freezer. "It's almost dinnertime. Only half an hour."

Hoby slammed the freezer shut. "Okay. Sorry, Mom. I'm just really hungry." He was glad to see that she had taken the football helmet off.

"Have an apple. That should hold you until dinner," his mom told him.

"Right." Hoby grabbed an apple and raced out the door.

As he took the back steps two at a time, he heard a crash behind him. One of his mom's flowerpots had smashed on the ground.

"Oh, guns! Sorry about that," Zirc said.

"Guns?"

"I know. I'm not allowed to curse either. But sometimes I can't help it," Zirc said.

"Is guns a curse word in your time?" Hoby asked.

"Yeah. But it's not as bad as the W word," Zirc told him.

"What's the W word?" Hoby asked.

"War," Zirc whispered.

"Really? So you don't have wars anymore?"

"No. But we have IPS. It's pretty much the same thing, I think."

"What's IPS?"

"Interplanetary strife. Anyway, where's your mord so we can fix this?"

"My what?"

"Your mord. Molecular restructuring device. Don't tell me it hasn't been invented yet."

"I've never heard of a mord. What is it?" Hoby scooped up the pieces of the flowerpot and put them in a pile by the steps.

"Well, it's a little square thing with buttons. You aim it at whatever you've broken, punch in the material, and press the restructure button. It puts it back together, good as new."

"Wow. My mom would love it if we had one of those around here."

"Yeah. My mom would have disowned me by now if we didn't have one." Zirc looked sadly at the broken flowerpot. "Veeb, I've gotta be more careful."

"It's okay. My mom has lots of flowerpots. I'll clean up the broken one later," Hoby told him. "Come on. I want to see your space cruiser."

Zirc led him into the woods. They walked for a few minutes until they came to a strange-looking machine. It looked like a cross between a helicopter and a sports car. It was just big enough for two people to sit in.

"It's the newest model. My dad just got it a couple weeks ago. Zall, huh?" Zirc said.

"Yeah," Hoby said.

"It really cruises, too. You can get to the moon in forty-five minutes," Zirc told him.

"Really? The moon?"

"Yup. Fastest cruiser around. My dad will strangle me if he finds out I took it. Luckily he and my mom are away for the next few days. They took my sister to Jupiter to look at the university there."

"Uh-huh," Hoby said. Maybe this wasn't a dream. But if it wasn't a dream, that meant one of two things. Either Hoby had gone crazy, or Zirc was real. He didn't think he was crazy, but could a person be the judge of his own sanity? Maybe he was crazy and didn't know it.

Now he almost hoped that Zirc was real. For one thing, he didn't want to be crazy. And for another, if Zirc was real, it was the most exciting thing that had happened in ages, a real live boy all the way from the next millennium, right here in his own backyard.

Hoby walked around the space cruiser, looking at it and touching it.

"You want to sit in it?" Zirc asked.

Hoby thought about it. He would have liked to have seen what it was like to sit inside a space cruiser, but he didn't want to end up in the next millennium.

"Um, maybe later," he told Zirc. "But right now I gotta go home for dinner."

"Oh," Zirc said. "Well, come on back out after dinner."

"Yeah, maybe. But I've got a ton of homework, so I might have to wait until tomorrow. I'll definitely see you tomorrow after school, though. And I'll keep an eye on that battery for you. How long till it charges?"

"Seventy-two hours," Zirc told him.

"Okay, well, see you tomorrow."

"Sure."

Hoby ran across his backyard and burst into the kitchen.

"There you are, Hoby," his mom said. "Dinner's almost ready. Go wash up and then set the table, please."

"Right, Mom, but first I gotta ask you something. Do you think I've been acting normal lately?"

His mother smiled. "It depends on what you mean by normal, Hoby."

"I mean, you know, regular. The way I always act."

"I haven't seen any major change in your behavior, if that's what you're asking."

"So I haven't been acting crazy or—or mentally ill or anything?" Hoby asked.

"No more so than you usually do." She laughed.

"Mom, I'm serious. Just tell me the truth."

"Hoby, I don't think you're crazy. You might be a little anxious right now. I guess we all are. Having a baby is a big change for a family. It's very normal for you to feel anxiety, and to have conflicting emotions and—"

"Right, right. Anxiety, but nothing more than that. No personality change, no really weird behavior?"

"No, Hoby. You are just fine. And I wouldn't change a thing about you," she said, giving him a hug. "Except possibly that shirt. It's filthy. Now go get ready for dinner and quit worrying so much."

Hoby went upstairs. His mom didn't think he was crazy. He didn't feel crazy. And Taz had seen Zirc, too. He and Taz couldn't both be crazy, could they? And Hammerhead! Hoby remembered that Hammerhead had seen Zirc. So Hoby wasn't imagining it. Zirc was real.

Hoby pulled on a clean T-shirt.

Zirc's green jumpsuit lay on the floor beside the bed. Taz sprawled on it.

"We've got a real live time traveler visiting us. That's something, huh?"

"Yeah a yeah a yeah," said Taz.

chapter five

After dinner, Hoby was back in his room when he heard something tapping on his window. Taz poked his head out from underneath Hoby's desk and looked up.

"Yeah, I heard it, boy," Hoby told him, looking through the glass.

There was Zirc, squatting on the roof right outside.

Hoby slid the window open and Zirc climbed into the room, rubbing his arms and puffing. "It's getting cold out there," Zirc said. "It never gets this cold in my time in September."

"Really? Global warming, I guess," Hoby said.

"Nah. Atmo-stasis. Weather control. Almost

all cities and towns have it. It's zall except when the system breaks down. Then things get really razzed up."

Zirc sat down on Hoby's lower bunk. "Veeb, your neighbor is one galactic dworb."

"You mean Hammerhead?" Hoby asked.

"Big kid? Bulgy red eyes?"

"That's him," Hoby said. "Hammerhead Jones. Well, his real name is Harold, but we call him Hammerhead."

"Well, I'd stay away from him if I were you," Zirc said.

"Staying away from Hammerhead is my life's ambition," Hoby said. "Unfortunately, it's not that easy."

"I know what you mean. He's out there now, walking his dog. Seems like he's looking for me. This afternoon, before I followed you inside, he chased me around the block and threatened to make me into an apple pie. And he tried to take my battery away from me. All I was doing was picking some apples from the tree. There were plenty. I didn't think anyone would mind."

"There's nothing that Hammerhead doesn't mind," Hoby said. "It's a good thing he didn't get your battery."

"I'll say. It's safe in your freezer, right?"

"Oh yeah. It's fine. But I'm surprised Hammerhead went after you. I told him your dad was the new chief of police."

"You did? Thanks, Hoby. But I think he's mad at me because I threw that apple at him."

"You threw an apple at him? When?" Hoby asked.

"This afternoon when he was about to pound you. Splat. Hit him right on the ear," Zirc said proudly.

"That was you? Great shot!"

"Yeah, but I gotta tell you," Zirc said, "I got enough problems as it is. The last thing I need is that dworb after me. I'm stuck here till my battery charges, no place to sleep, nothing to eat, and my parents are going to murder me if I don't get back before they do." Zirc sighed. "I wish I'd never pushed that button."

"I could get you some food," Hoby offered. "Maybe you'll feel better after you eat."

Zirc looked up. "Could you? That'd be zall. I'm so hungry I'll eat anything. Even veggie pellets or seaweed burgers, which I usually hate."

"How about a peanut butter and jelly sandwich?" Hoby asked.

"Zall."

Hoby's mom was just coming out of the kitchen. "Oh, Hoby. You scared me," she said when she saw him.

"Sorry, Mom," he said. His mom stopped, blocking his way into the kitchen. She had her hands behind her back. Hoby had a feeling he knew why.

"Uh, Mom, what's that you've got behind your back?"

"Behind my back? Nothing at all. See?" she said, bringing out one hand and leaning against the wall.

"I believe you have two hands, Mom. Most people do."

"Yes, I do, and here's the other one. See?" she said brightly, putting the first hand behind her back and showing him the other.

"Mom. It's chocolate, isn't it?"

"Hoby, I couldn't help myself. I just had this terrible, terrible craving. One little bag of chocolate-covered peanuts won't hurt anything, will it, Hoby? I mean, they're mostly peanuts. There's really not much chocolate at all."

"Mom, what about our pact?"

Hoby wasn't supposed to chew gum because of his braces, and his mom wasn't supposed to eat chocolate because she didn't think it was good for the baby.

"I know, Hoby. I feel terrible. And you've been so good about the gum."

"I'll tell you what, Mom. Why don't you give me half? I'm sure half a bag of them can't hurt anything."

"That seems fair," she said. She poured half the bag into Hoby's hands.

"Don't feel too bad, Mom. When Barney's mom was pregnant she once ate seven chocolate donuts in a row."

"Goodness. Seven?"

"That's what Barney said."

Hoby made some sandwiches and took them up to Zirc. The phone rang, and Hoby picked it up.

"That you, wimp?"

"Yeah, it's me, Harold," Hoby said.

"Uh-oh," Zirc whispered.

"Guess what I found out," Hammerhead went on.

"Um, I'm kind of busy right now, Harold. I've got a lot of homework," Hoby said.

"Yeah, well, maybe I'll just tell you then. I found out that the new police chief doesn't have any children."

"Is that a f-fact?" Hoby said.

"That's a fact, all right. Which means you lied to me today."

"I wouldn't call it lying, Harold. It was a mistake. Everyone makes mistakes now and then."

"Do you know what happens to people who lie to me?" Hammerhead growled.

"But Harold—"

"People who lie to me, I like to think of them as bread dough."

"B-bread dough?" Hoby said.

"Have you ever made bread?" Hammerhead asked.

"N-no," Hoby said.

"It involves a lot of kneading, pounding, flattening, and punching. I think I'm going to be making some bread tomorrow afternoon." Clunk. Hammerhead hung up.

"What'd he say?" Zirc asked.

"He was talking about making bread," Hoby told him.

"Making bread? You're telling me that this Hammerhead called to exchange recipes? That's kind of hard to believe," Zirc said.

"He's planning to use me as the dough," Hoby told him.

"Oh," Zirc said.

"He found out I lied to him about your being the police chief's son."

"Look, Hoby. Hammerhead's out to get both of us, but between the two of us we should be able to get the best of him. Especially if I'm invisible."

Hoby looked at Zirc. A small flame of hope flickered inside him. "That could help," he said.

"What time do you get home from school? I'll meet you on the corner, and when Hammerhead shows up, I'll dematerialize and we'll take him by surprise."

"It might work," Hoby said. "Meet me there at three-fifteen."

"I'll be there," Zirc said, nodding. "But I sure hope I get some sleep tonight. That hammock's not the greatest place to spend the night."

Hoby thought of Zirc sleeping in the hammock. It would be cold, not to mention scary, all alone out there in the dark. Hoby couldn't tell his parents about Zirc, but he was pretty sure they wouldn't want him sleeping outside, especially when Hoby had a perfectly good bunk bed going to waste.

"Can you be invisible in your sleep?" Hoby asked.

"Sure, I just set my dematerializer for sleep mode, and I'll stay invisible until I reset it in the morning."

"Why don't you just stay here, then? If you're invisible no one will know, and it'll be a lot more comfortable than the hammock."

"You mean it?" Zirc asked.

Hoby shrugged. "Yeah."

He was glad that Zirc was staying. Hoby liked him, and Zirc understood about Hammerhead. Maybe together they really could put an end to his bullying.

chapter six

The next day Hoby walked home from school with Patrick and Patience.

"Let's go to the tree house," Patience said. Patrick and Patience lived two blocks away from Hoby. They had a tree house in their backyard where the three of them spent lots of afternoons.

"I can't. I've got to get home," Hoby said.

"Why?"

"I can't tell you right now. I'll explain later," Hoby told them.

"Wait a minute," Patience said. "You can't tell someone you have a secret but not tell what it is. It's not fair. We'll be imagining all kinds of things."

"You'll never imagine the truth," Hoby said with a smile.

"Okay. That's it. Now you really have to tell us," Patrick said.

Hoby wanted to tell them. He was dying to tell them. He couldn't keep it inside any longer. Zirc wouldn't mind. After all, Patrick and Patience were his best friends.

"I'll tell you what. Come with me to the corner of my street and you can see it for yourselves," Hoby said.

"Let's go," Patience said.

This is gonna be great, Hoby told himself.

When they got to the corner, Hoby looked at his watch. It was exactly three-fifteen.

"We're right on time," he said.

"On time for what, Hobe? Where's the big secret?" Patrick asked.

"He'll be here soon," Hoby told them.

"Who will be here?" Patience asked.

"Zirc. He's going to meet us here at three-fifteen."

"Who is this Zirc?" Patrick asked.

"You'll meet him in a minute," Hoby said.

But several minutes passed, and there was no sign of Zirc. Where was he? He should have come by now. Maybe he was invisible. Maybe he was scared of Patrick and Patience. Maybe he didn't want them to know about him. "Zirc?" Hoby called. "It's okay, Zirc. These are my friends."

"I don't see anyone, Hobe. You sure he's coming?" Patrick shot a skeptical look at Patience.

"Zirc? Zirc? Are you here, Zirc?" Hoby turned in circles and waved his arms.

"Hey, maybe he just forgot, Hobe," Patience said.

"No. You don't understand. See, he's invisible," Hoby tried to explain. "He might be here right now." Hoby spun and waved his arms even harder. "Zirc? You promised you'd be here. You don't have to materialize, Zirc. Just give us a sign that you're here."

Patrick whispered something to Patience and then turned to Hoby. "Um. You say this friend of yours is invisible, Hoby?"

"Right. He's invisible. Not always, but some of the time. *Zirc?* Where are you? I don't understand this. He promised he'd be here."

Patrick and Patience were whispering again. "So, this friend of yours is invisible some of the time, but not always. And where did you say you met him?" Patience asked.

"He was in our hammock yesterday morning. Then later he was in the bathroom," Hoby told them. "And then he was on the roof outside my window."

"In the hammock, in the bathroom, and on the roof outside your window . . . uh-huh. And he's invisible?" Patience said.

"Yes, yes, he's . . . see, he's from the next millennium. Oh, I told you you'd never believe it. I just wish he'd show up so you could see for yourselves."

Patrick and Patience exchanged a look. "Uh-huh. And how often do you see this, ah, Zirc?" Patrick asked.

They think I'm crazy, Hoby realized. Of course they would. Who would believe it? And where was Zirc? Had something happened to him?

"Look, Hobe, I know you're upset about this thing with Hammerhead, but you've got to calm down. Take it easy. Everything's okay, really," Patience said.

"But it's not okay," Hoby screamed. "He's supposed to be here. *Zirc! Where are you, Zirc?*"

chapter seven

Hoby couldn't stand the way Patrick and Patience were looking at him. Without another word he raced up the street, leaving the twins on the corner, staring after him. He was fishing in his pocket for his house key when his mother opened the door.

"Mom, you're home? I thought you were going to be at the office all day today."

"Well, I decided to come home early today, Hoby. I just had this urge to clean. It must be the nesting instinct."

"The nesting instinct?" Hoby said.

"Yes. They say it happens to pregnant women. You get an urge to clean everything and get your house all ready for the new baby, just like birds making nests for their eggs."

"Oh." Maybe that's why Zirc hadn't shown up, Hoby thought. Maybe he was afraid to come out because he didn't want Hoby's mother to see him. But why hadn't he just dematerialized? No one, not even his mother, who had always amazed Hoby with her ability to see things when he was sure she wasn't looking, could see Zirc when he was invisible.

"Yes," Hoby's mother went on happily. "And I got so much done. I got the refrigerator and the freezer all cleaned out. They sure needed it."

"That's goo— Uh, did you say the freezer?" Hoby asked.

"Uh-huh. All that old stuff. Some of it's been there so long I didn't even know what it was. I put it all right in the trash, and the trash men will take it away tomorrow."

Hoby ran into the kitchen and pulled open the freezer door. There was nothing in there but ice trays and a few boxes of frozen food, neatly stacked. He looked behind them in the back where he had hidden Zirc's battery. Nothing. What if he lost the battery? Zirc would never be able to get home again.

He raced outside to the garbage cans.

He pulled the top off the first can and had just started plowing through the garbage when Hammerhead appeared. "Looking for something, Hobson?"

Hammerhead was holding Zirc's battery. "I saw your friend with this the other day. When I saw it in your garbage, I thought it was something he'd want back."

"Yeah. My friend would do anything to get it back, so . . . " Hoby stopped. This was not a normal person who would return a valuable item to its rightful owner. No. This was Hammerhead.

"Anything, huh? Then the little favor I'm going to ask shouldn't be any problem at all," Hammerhead said.

"What kind of favor?" Hoby asked.

"Just a matter of getting a copy of the answer sheet to Mr. Epstein's seventh-grade math test."

"Look, Harold. I—I don't know, I mean, I don't know how my friend would feel about—"

Hammerhead clamped a huge meaty hand on Hoby's shoulder and squeezed. "Remember what we talked about last night?"

"About b-bread making?" Hoby asked.

"Right. About how it involves a lot of kneading"—squeeze—"flattening"—squeeze—"and pounding"—squeeze squeeze.

"Y-yeah," Hoby said.

"Well, if your friend wants his battery back and you don't want to be bread dough, figure out a way to get that test."

Hammerhead let go of him and stomped off with Zirc's battery. Hoby rubbed his shoulder, wondering if there were any broken bones.

"Harold," Hoby called.

"Yeah?"

"The battery. It needs to be kept in a freezer."

"I'll take care of it," Hammerhead said.

Hoby's heart sank. He had promised Zirc that the battery was safe. How was he going to break the news that now it was in the hands of a galactic dworb?

chapter eight

Hoby raced upstairs and burst into his room. Zirc was lying on the bunk bed, reading a comic book.

"What happened? I thought you were going to meet me on the corner," Hoby said.

"I couldn't. Your mom came home just as I was about to leave, and the timer on my dematerializer isn't working again. I was afraid she'd see me."

Zirc sat up. "I think I could fix this dematerializer if I had a laser rod. Do you have one?"

"We've got screwdrivers. You think that would do it?"

Zirc shrugged. "It's worth a try, I guess."

"I'll get you one from my dad's workshop. But listen, I've got some really bad news." Hoby took a deep breath.

"Yeah? What?" Zirc asked.

"Well, see, my mom's got this thing called a nesting instinct. It makes her want to clean. So she decided to clean out the freezer. She threw out your battery—"

"What?" Zirc cried, jumping up off the bed. "Threw it out where? We've got to get it!"

"No, it's okay. It's not in the garbage anymore."

"Then where is it? Is it back in the freezer?"

"It's in a freezer, but not our freezer."

"Hoby, whose freezer is it in?"

"Hammerhead's," Hoby said miserably.

Zirc stared at Hoby, his eyes large and round. The blood drained from his face. "I don't think I heard you right. Did you just tell me that Hammerhead has my battery?"

Hoby nodded.

"The Hammerhead with the bulgy red eyes? The Hammerhead who chased me around the block? The Hammerhead who is going to pound you into bread dough and make me into an apple pie? That Hammerhead?"

Hoby nodded. "There's only one Hammerhead," he said, "which is good, because if there were more than one, it would be—"

"*Hoby!*" Zirc shouted, collapsing into Hoby's desk chair. "My little sister's birthday is in two days. How do you think she'll feel if her big brother is gone? Vanished into thin air along with her father's space cruiser? How do you think my mother will feel when she says, 'Yes, I used to have a son. His name was Zirc. But he disappeared.' How do you think my flizball team will feel when they realize one of their star players is never coming back?"

"Look, Zirc. We'll get the battery back. I promise you. In fact, Hammerhead is planning to give it back."

Zirc sat up. "He is? When?"

"As soon as we do one simple favor. All we have to do is get something for him."

"Well, let's go get it. Come on, the sooner the better."

"Well, it's a little more complicated than that. It's the answer sheet for a test."

"A test? What's a test?" Zirc asked.

"A test is, um, well, it's something you have to take in school to prove that you learned stuff. Don't you have tests?"

"We don't have tests but we've got knaps— knowledge appraisals. We have little machines called knaplers. They ask questions, and we say the answers into the machines. But we're not allowed to see the answers before we take the knap, 'cause that wouldn't be fair."

"Yeah, I know."

"Hoby, if a test is like a knap, it seems pretty obvious why Hammerhead wants the answers," Zirc said. "Maybe schools are different back in these days, but at my school that would be called cheating. I don't think we should help someone be a cheater."

"Believe me, I don't either," Hoby said. "Do you think I want to help Hammerhead? I've never cheated in my life, and I wouldn't, but we've got to get a copy of that answer sheet. It's the only way."

"Yeah, I guess we don't have any choice. I've got to get my battery back."

"And, if you're invisible, it won't be that hard," Hoby said.

"But the first thing we have to do is fix the timer on my dematerializer."

"Yeah, I'll go get you a screwdriver."

"Okay, and I'll clean up your room," Zirc said. "Where's your robo-cleaner?"

"My what?"

"Your robo-cleaner. It's a little machine that cleans for you. It can vacuum, put stuff away, and hang up clothes in about thirty seconds. Every room has one, and they're programmed so they know where everything goes."

"I wish I had one, but we have to do it the old-fashioned way," Hoby said.

Zirc started picking up the comics and books. "Veeb, this is hard work."

"I'll be right back," Hoby said. He went downstairs and out to his father's workshop. He found a screwdriver and put it in his pocket just as Patrick and Patience came through the gate into the backyard.

"Hey, Hobe," Patrick said cheerfully. "What's up?"

"Hoby! Hi," Patience said. She held up a bag. "Look. We brought you some cookies. Are you feeling okay?"

"I'm fine," Hoby said.

"Great. That's great, Hobe."

"Why are you being like that?" Hoby asked.

"Like what?" she asked innocently.

"Nice," Hoby said.

"I'm not being nice. Am I being nice, Patrick? I'm just being regular."

"You brought me cookies," Hoby said. "You never give away cookies."

"These are burnt. They're really not very good at all, are they, Patrick?"

Patrick turned a cookie over and said, "See? The bottoms are burnt. She's trying to get rid of them, that's all."

"No, no, we're not being nice. We're just being regular. Regular old Patrick and regular old Patience," Patience assured Hoby.

"Well, that's good. Want to come up to my room?" Hoby asked. Zirc was waiting for him in his room. Patrick and Patience would finally see that Zirc was real. They followed Hoby inside.

"Actually, there is someone I want you to meet," Hoby said as he opened the door to his room.

"Oh yeah? Who's that?" Patrick asked.

"Zirc?" Hoby said, looking around the room. He must be invisible again, Hoby realized. "Zirc, here's Patrick and Patience. Remember I told you about them? And I got the screwdriver. You can fix the dematerializer now." Hoby held out the screwdriver. "Zirc? Are you in here?"

Patrick glanced at Patience. "Not this again," Hoby heard him whisper.

"Zirc? It's okay. They want to meet you."

Then Patrick clapped Hoby on the back. "Hey, it's okay, man. We can meet him later, you know? Right, Patience?"

"Right," Patience said. "Definitely. I'm really not in the mood to meet anyone right now, anyway. Are you, Patrick?"

"Zirc! Don't do this to me again, Zirc. Where are you?" Hoby shouted. He waved his arms.

Patrick shook his head. "No. I definitely don't want to meet anyone right now. Bad idea. Another time, Hobe. Don't worry about it."

"But he was just here," Hoby cried. He sat down on his bed. "Really. He was cleaning up my room while I went to get the screwdriver."

Patrick and Patience stared at him.

"We've got to humor him," Patience whispered to Patrick. She sat down next to Hoby. "Hoby, this Zirc. Is he the one you saw in your hammock and then in your bathroom? And on the roof?"

"Yes. And he was supposed to meet me on the corner, but his dematerializer got broken."

"Um, Hobe, have you told anyone else about this Zirc?"

"No. I'm not supposed to tell anyone. Not even you, but you guys are my best friends, so I wanted you to know about him."

"That's right, Hoby. It's probably best if you don't mention Zirc to anyone else. But we are your best friends. And we want to help you. We really do, don't we, Patrick?"

"Of course. That's what friends are for, Hobe."

"And I've known other people who've had friends like Zirc," said Patience.

"Really? You have?" Hoby asked.

"Sure. Lots of kids have invisible friends. They're usually a little younger than you, but that's okay. If it makes you feel better to have an imaginary, I mean, an invisible friend, well, it's fine by us."

"Zirc is real, he's not just in my imagination," Hoby yelled. "Just forget I ever mentioned it. I got a lot of homework, so maybe you guys should go."

"Okay," Patience said, "but if you feel the need to talk about Zirc, we're here for you. Any time, right, Patrick?"

"Right. Of course. We're here for you, buddy."

"Great. I'll see you later," Hoby said as they left.

"And, Hoby?" Patience called in her sickeningly sweet voice. "Remember, other people might get the wrong idea if you tell them about Zirc, so let's just keep him our secret, okay?"

When they were gone, there was a zap and Zirc appeared.

"Where've you been?" Hoby asked.

"Invisible. I told you I don't want anyone to know about me."

"But they're my best friends."

"I don't care. I don't want them to know."

"Great. Now my best friends really think I'm nuts."

chapter nine

The next morning, Hoby looked at himself in the mirror. There was nothing special about his face. It was ordinary, average. The only thing it had in its favor was that it had an honest sort of look. It was a face most people would trust. Stealing the answers to a math test was not something this face would normally do. But this was not a normal situation. If they didn't get the answers, Zirc would be stuck a millennium away from home, and Hoby would be pounded into bread dough by Hammerhead. And as ordinary as it was, he didn't want his face turned into dough.

Last night after Zirc had fixed the timer on the dematerializer, they had talked about their plan.

It was foolproof. Hoby was sure that everything would work out, but still, he would be glad when it was over.

Hoby was brushing his teeth when he heard a scream from his bedroom. He flew out of the bathroom and found his mother in the hall with a pile of clean laundry. "Hoby, there's something in your room. A mouse or something."

Uh-oh, Hoby thought.

"Are you sure it wasn't Taz?"

"No. I'm positive I saw something moving in there, and it wasn't Taz. He's still asleep on your bed. There's something in the top bunk. Really. I'm sure I saw it." Hoby went into his room and stripped the sheets back, praying that Zirc would know enough to keep still and quiet.

"There's nothing there, Mom."

"But . . . I'm sure I . . . maybe it was the wind, but really . . . "

"Whew. That was close," Hoby whispered as soon as his mom had left his room. "Zirc? Zirc?" Now what? Hoby thought. Where was he?

"Aaahhhh!" There was a crash and then a scream from the bathroom. "Hoby, that mouse is in the bathroom now," his mom said as he ran in. "I was putting the clean towels away, and something knocked a bottle of shampoo off the shelf onto the floor."

Hoby glanced around the bathroom. "Well, I don't see anything, Mom. You seem really jumpy this morning. Are you sure you're feeling okay?"

Hoby went back into his own room and closed the door. "Zirc?" he whispered. "Are you in here?"

"Yeah, I'm here." There was a zap, and a disheveled Zirc materialized. "I gotta tell you, this is not a good way to wake up."

"I know. Look, I'm going to get breakfast. I'll bring you some toast," Hoby said.

"Yeah, that'd be zall. I'm starved," Zirc said.

Hoby ran down to the kitchen. He ate a bowl of cereal and grabbed two pieces of toast, being careful not to let his mother see him take them up to his room.

"Come on," he told Zirc as he handed him the toast. "We've got to hurry, or I'll be late for school."

Zirc pressed his dematerializer and vanished.

"Is the timer fixed?" Hoby asked.

"I think so. It's working now, anyway."

As they turned into the gates to school, Hoby said, "So you've got the plan, right? And in case we get separated at school, you can meet me in my homeroom. It's room 206." Suddenly Hoby felt a hand on his shoulder.

"Hello, Hoby dear." It was Ms. Tinsley, the school guidance counselor.

"Oh, hi, Ms. Tinsley," Hoby said. Ms. Tinsley was a small woman with gray hair and round wire-rim glasses. She always wore pins and buttons with inspirational sayings on them—WE'RE ALL IN THIS TOGETHER or LET'S TALK ABOUT IT—kind of like a walking bumper sticker. She smiled a lot when she spoke to him, but Hoby had the feeling she was studying him as if he were an interesting new kind of fungus she had discovered.

"I see that you're talking to yourself, Hoby. Having quite a conversation by the look of it," she said.

"Um, I was rehearsing some lines for my part in a play," he told her.

"I see. And which play would that be, dear?"

"Um, well, it's just a skit for English class."

"I see. Well, very good. Don't let me interrupt you."

As they went into the school building, Hoby whispered to Zirc, "Just try to stay with me, okay, Zirc? Zirc?" He saw that Ms. Tinsley was still watching him, and he smiled and waved.

"Don't worry. I'll stay with you," Zirc whispered.

"And remember, you're invisible. You've got to be quiet or you'll scare people to death," Hoby hissed.

In his first period history class, there were two empty seats beside Patrick. Hoby took one and hoped that Zirc would take the other.

As Hoby got out his notebook, there was a loud squeak from Zirc's desk, and it slid toward Hoby. From behind them Carrie Bateman gave a little cry.

"Quiet. You're invisible," Hoby whispered, nudging Zirc with his elbow.

"Ow," Zirc said.

Mr. Pringle looked up from his desk. Hoby began rubbing his elbow.

"A problem, Mr. Hobson?"

"No, no problem, sir. I just hit my elbow, is all."

"I'm sorry to hear that, Mr. Hobson. Do you think we can make it through the rest of class without any more outbursts?"

"Yes sir."

Carrie raised her hand.

"Yes, Miss Bateman?"

"My desk squeaks. Can I move?"

"Move to the empty desk in front of you."

Carrie gathered up her books. In a minute she would be sitting on Zirc's lap.

"No!" Hoby shouted. "It's not, um, I mean . . . it's not safe."

"Not safe?" Mr. Pringle was looking at Hoby as if he'd lost his mind.

"The seat is loose." Hoby grabbed the chair and yanked it back and forth. "I tried to sit there and almost fell. It's very dangerous, really."

"Maybe I could just sit over next to Dana," said Carrie. Hoby noticed that she was looking at him in a very strange way. There was a funny expression in her eyes and a silly sort of smile on her lips.

"That's fine, Miss Bateman. Now, class, let's get started. Please take out your notebooks." Hoby tried to take notes on what Mr. Pringle was saying, but Zirc's seat began swinging from side to side.

"Stop it," Hoby whispered, giving Zirc a kick beneath the desk.

"Ow!" Zirc shouted.

"Mr. Hobson? Another problem? You seem to be having a very difficult morning."

"Yes sir. It's my stomach. Could I be excused to go to the boys' room?"

"By all means."

"Come on," he whispered to Zirc.

In the hall Hoby stopped. "Zirc?"

"Yeah, I'm right here."

"Whew. I thought Carrie was going to sit right on top of you." Hoby laughed until he saw Ms. Tinsley staring at him from her office across the hall.

chapter
ten

It was lunch period. Hoby would wait until everyone had gone to the cafeteria, and then he and Zirc would put their plan into action. As he was waiting by his locker, Carrie came up to him.

"Hoby, you were so sweet to be so worried about me sitting in that dangerous desk in history class," she said. "Honestly, I didn't know you cared." She blinked her eyes at him.

"Uh, well, I wouldn't want anyone getting hurt, is all," Hoby told her.

"Of course you wouldn't," she said, looking at him as if he were a hot fudge sundae she was about to bite into.

"Uh, I gotta go, Carrie," he said.

"Aren't you coming to lunch?" she asked.

"I gotta do something first."

"Well, I'll save you a seat."

"Yeah. Great."

Finally the halls were clear. "Okay, remember," Hoby said to Zirc. "The seventh-grade answer sheet is right in there on Mr. Epstein's desk. All you have to do is get it, take it right down the hall here to the copy room, make a copy, and then return the original to the desk. Then you give the copy to me and head for home. Simple, right?"

"I don't know. I mean, what if I get caught?"

"How can you get caught? You're invisible."

"But I just don't like the idea of taking the answer sheet," Zirc said.

"I don't like it either, but what choice do we have? Besides, we're not going to use it. It's for Hammerhead. You want your battery back, don't you? This is self-defense."

"Okay. Let's get it over with," Zirc said.

Hoby waited outside Mr. Epstein's room while Zirc went in to get the answer sheet.

Please don't let Mrs. Stoutwell come back early, he prayed. He hadn't said anything about her to Zirc because he didn't want to worry him, but Mrs. Stoutwell could be a problem.

Mrs. Stoutwell was the school secretary. She considered the copy room her kingdom and the copy machine her most prized possession. Students were not supposed to use it at all, unless they filled out all kinds of forms. Even the teachers were scared of her. Once she had made Ms. Treemer, the music teacher, cry, and another time she gave Mr. Jackson, the gym teacher, detention. Mrs. Stoutwell would not be happy if she came back from lunch and heard someone using her copy machine.

The classroom door opened and Hoby saw a white piece of paper float by. In a minute he heard the copy machine start. Everything was going perfectly. Soon it would all be over.

Hoby stood at his post, watching and listening. The copy machine kept running. It shouldn't take so long to make just one copy, should it? Finally Hoby ran into the copy room.

A sea of white paper covered the floor, and Zirc stood staring helplessly as the machine continued to crank out paper after paper.

"What happened? And why aren't you invisible?" Hoby asked.

"I can't stop it! It's gone crazy. I had to materialize. My fingers don't work as well when I'm invisible."

"Oh, gosh, we've got to stop it and get this cleaned up fast."

Zirc punched the stop button over and over. "I took the answer sheet out so the papers are just blank, but it won't stop."

Hoby found the electric cord and gave it a yank. Finally, the machine cranked to a halt. Hoby put the answer sheet and the copy for Hammerhead into his notebook.

Then he sprang into action, scooping up the papers and shoving them into the wastebasket as fast as he could. "Come on. If Mrs. Stoutwell catches us, we've had it."

"Who's Mrs.—" The door burst open, and there stood Mrs. Stoutwell.

"What in heaven's name is going on in here, Hoby?" Mrs. Stoutwell boomed. "And who is this? Is he a new student?"

"Mrs. Stoutwell, this is my cousin Zirc from Ohio. He's here visiting us, and my mom thought it would be fun for him to come to school with me today. So he could, sort of, you know, see what another school is like, and so he came with me and here we are and . . . "

Mrs. Stoutwell nodded. "That doesn't explain what the two of you are doing in my copy room, and why it's in such a mess."

"I was just trying to make a copy of, um, m-my schedule for Zirc, Mrs. Stoutwell, and the machine got stuck."

"Hoby, you are well aware that no one is allowed to touch my copy machine without my permission. I suggest we pay a visit to Mr. Seymour, and you explain it all to him."

"B-but Mrs. Stoutwell—" Hoby said, but one look at Mrs. Stoutwell's face told him there was no point in going on.

"What did you say your name was, young man?" Mrs. Stoutwell asked Zirc as they marched down the hall to Mr. Seymour's office.

"Zirc. Zircus Orflandu."

"My, that's an unusual name."

"It's, um, Belgian," Hoby told her.

Zirc was fiddling with his dematerializer band. "What's wrong?" Hoby whispered.

"The timer's stuck again. It's set to dematerialize me in five minutes, and I can't get it unstuck."

"You can't dematerialize in the middle of Mr. Seymour's office."

"All I can do is put it on slow mode. I'll start getting pale and finally just fade out. If you see that happening, get us out of there."

chapter eleven

As principals went, Mr. Seymour was okay. He was a little man with a bald head and a round, wrinkled face. His back was slightly stooped, and he had a favorite green jacket that he wore almost every day. Kids called him the turtle because he moved and spoke with extreme slowness. When Mrs. Stoutwell hauled students into his office by their ears, Mr. Seymour always acted happy to see them, as if they were paying him a social call.

It was well known that Mr. Seymour was just as terrified of Mrs. Stoutwell as everyone else was, but he was completely dependent on her because she had been there so long. She knew things that no one else knew, like how to work the PA system and how to adjust the clocks. The truth was, Mrs. Stoutwell ran the school, and Mr. Seymour did pretty much whatever she told him to do. But when she sent students to his office, most of the time all Mr. Seymour did was talk to them for a while and then let them go. That was the thing about Mr. Seymour. He loved to talk.

When Mrs. Stoutwell appeared in his office with Hoby and Zirc, Mr. Seymour rose slowly and came out from behind his desk to greet them. "Ah, Mrs. Stoutwell. You've brought me some visitors?"

"Hoby Hobson and his cousin from Ohio. I found them in my copy room." She paused to let this sink in, and Mr. Seymour seemed to shrink slightly. Hoby felt that at any moment his head might disappear down inside his green jacket. "You know how I feel about students touching my copy machine, Mr. Seymour."

Mr. Seymour nodded slowly. "I will have . . . a nice . . . long chat with them, Mrs. Stoutwell. You may rest assured."

"I can assure you I will not be resting, Mr. Seymour. If you could see the pile of work on my desk, you would know I will not be resting," she said, glaring at Hoby.

"Merely . . . a figure . . . of speech, Mrs. Stoutwell. I of . . . all . . . people . . . am well aware that . . . your work leaves . . . you little time for rest." He placed a hand on her elbow and steered her gently toward the door, like a little tugboat piloting a barge out of the harbor.

He closed the door behind her and turned to Hoby and Zirc. "Sit, boys. Please sit," he said. Hoby and Zirc sat down in the two chairs that faced Mr. Seymour's desk and waited while he made his way back to his own chair. "Well," he said. "Hoby, you are certainly an old friend, but I don't believe I've met your cousin before. Are you a new student, my boy?"

"No sir," Zirc said.

"He's just visiting, sir," Hoby said. "From Ohio."

"I see. Just visiting," Mr. Seymour said, nodding.

Hoby looked at his watch. How long did they have until Zirc's timer went off and he started to fade? "Um, actually, sir, we haven't had lunch yet, and we wouldn't want to be late for science class, which starts in just a few minutes," Hoby said.

"Science class. Yes, that's very . . . important, of course." Mr. Seymour nodded. "I commend you for wanting to be punctual . . . and, ordinarily, of course, the last thing . . . I would encourage you to do is to miss lunch, but you see, I really feel . . . we need to get to the bottom of this . . . copy room problem."

"Yes sir," said Hoby.

"It would be helpful . . . if you . . . could tell me . . . just exactly what you were doing in the copy room."

"We were copying," said Zirc.

"And you did, of course . . . have all . . . the forms necessary for using the copy machine?"

"Well, not exactly," said Hoby.

"Not exactly. Not exactly." Mr. Seymour nodded. "You mean, you had some but not all of the forms?"

"Well, actually, it was sort of an emergency."

"An emergency. Ah!"

Zirc and Hoby nodded.

"So after making this . . . emergency . . . trip to the copy room . . . " continued Mr. Seymour, "I gather that there were some problems?"

"Well, the machine got stuck, sort of, and we couldn't stop it and . . . " Hoby looked over at Zirc. He was getting paler. Hoby had to do something fast. "And speaking of emergencies." Hoby jumped up. "I, um, I have to go to the bathroom really badly."

Mr. Seymour nodded slowly. "You may be excused for a moment. Your cousin and I will wait here for you."

"But—but he's the one who has to go. He's—he's not feeling well, right, Zirc?"

Zirc nodded.

Mr. Seymour looked at Zirc. "He does look rather . . . pale. Perhaps you should take him to the nurse, and we will continue . . . our discussion . . . at a later time."

"Yes. The nurse. We better go right away." Hoby grabbed Zirc and hustled him out of Mr. Seymour's office.

As soon as they got out in the hall, there was a zap, and Zirc disappeared.

"Wow, that was close," Hoby said. "I thought you were going to dematerialize right there in his office." Hoby took the answer sheet out of his notebook. "Here. You've got to put this back on Mr. Epstein's desk right now, before he gets back from lunch. And don't let anyone see it."

Zirc took the answer sheet. "I'll put it under my sweatshirt. Then it will be invisible too," he said.

Hoby was still talking to Zirc when Ms. Tinsley came around the corner. She gave Hoby another strange look and said, "Hoby, dear? Do you find you talk to yourself like this a lot? Not that there's anything wrong with it, of course. Some people find it helps them to organize their thoughts. But it can be a sign of stress."

Hoby didn't know what to say, so he just nodded.

Patrick and Patience were right behind Ms. Tinsley. Patrick put his arm around Hoby's shoulder and said, "Hey, Hobe. How's it going? You been studying for that science test?" He looked at Ms. Tinsley. "He likes to study out loud, see, and it looks like he's talking to someone, but really he's just studying. Like you always tell us, Ms. Tinsley, we all need to develop our own unique study habits."

"Well, yes, that's true but . . . " She looked at Hoby with concern. "Perhaps you'd like to come in and discuss it with me in my office sometime, Hoby. We could talk about anything else that might be troubling you as well. Would you like that?"

"Don't you worry about Hoby, Ms. Tinsley. He's fine. Just dandy, right, Hobe?" Patrick said heartily.

"Um, ah, actually, I'm fine, Ms. Tinsley. But if I need to talk, I'll be sure to come and see you."

"Oh yes, Hoby. I'm here to listen," she said as she went on down the hall.

Patrick and Patience stood on either side of Hoby. They looked at each other across him.

"We wouldn't want to be mentioning your imaginary friend to Ms. Tinsley, Hobe," Patience said, "because see, well, you know how these psychologists are, always suspecting people of being crazy and all. We wouldn't want her to get the wrong idea, you know what I mean?"

As soon as he got rid of Patrick and Patience, Hoby hurried after Zirc, hoping he had put the answer sheet back on Mr. Epstein's desk in time. As he passed his locker on the way to his home-room, Hoby heard, "*Psst,* Hoby." It was Zirc.

"There you are. I've been waiting for you," Hoby said.

"You have?" said a voice. But this time it wasn't Zirc's voice. "Why, Hoby, that's just about the sweetest thing I've ever heard!"

Carrie Bateman beamed at him from across the block of lockers. "I looked for you in the lunchroom, but I didn't see you there," she told him. "Have you eaten yet? There are still a few minutes until the bell. You could go back and get something. I don't mind going with you." She smiled and blinked her eyes. He tried to think of a reason why he couldn't go to the lunchroom. Carrie grabbed her friend Sarah Louise and pulled her over beside them. "Sarah Louise will come with us, right, Sarah Louise?"

"But I just ate," Sarah Louise said.

Carrie yanked on Sarah Louise's arm and glared at her. "But Hoby wants us to come with him, don't you, Hoby?"

"I, um, uh." Before Hoby could finish Zirc, now materialized, came over to them and said, "Hi, Hobe. I'm starved. Let's go eat."

"Wait, I . . . ," Hoby began, but Carrie and Sarah Louise swept them along to the cafeteria.

"Did everything go okay with Mr. Epstein?" Hoby asked Zirc.

"All taken care of," Zirc told him.

Hoby breathed a sigh of relief. They had the copy of the answer sheet and the original was safely back on Mr. Epstein's desk. Tonight Zirc would get his battery back and everything would be fine.

As Hoby pushed his tray along the lunch counter, he saw something on Carrie's arm that sent fear blowing through his body like a cold wind. His hands grew clammy and his head felt light. Suddenly he wasn't hungry at all. The thing on her arm was a press-on tattoo. It was a picture of a heart with an arrow through it. Above the heart was written the initials C. B. and below it were the initials H. H. Don't panic, Hoby told himself. It was a big school. There were lots of kids with the initials H. H. Henry Hickman, for example. Probably the initials referred to Henry. Of course, Henry weighed about three hundred pounds and hadn't changed his shirt in two years. Somehow Hoby didn't think that Henry was Carrie's type, but still, there were other people with the initials H. H. Weren't there?

chapter twelve

As soon as they got home that afternoon, Hoby said, "Let's call Hammerhead and tell him to bring your battery back."

He took the answer sheet out of his notebook. "Yikes!" he said, staring at the copy. "Zirc, this is the wrong answer sheet. This is the one for the sixth-grade test. See, it says six right up here in the corner."

"The wrong answer sheet? You're kidding me."

"Hammerhead's not going to give the battery back when he sees this."

"Okay. Here's what we do," Zirc said. "We just change that six to a seven."

"He'll know as soon as he looks it over. He took sixth-grade math last year."

"Yeah, but maybe by the time he's had a chance to look it over, we'll have my battery back. One more night in the freezer and it'll be charged, and I can get home."

"Zirc, do you know what he'll do to us when he finds out we gave him the wrong answer sheet?" Hoby shivered.

"The minute we get the battery, we'll run into the house. And we'll make sure he can't follow us."

"How do we do that?"

"Do you have any phero-atomizing fluid?" Zirc asked.

"What's that?"

"It's stuff you spray and it sets up a force field barrier."

"Sounds cool. But we don't have that yet," Hoby told him.

"Hmmm. Well, what about something like this?" Zirc pulled out an old Archie comic book of Hoby's that he'd been reading and showed it to him. "Looks like this trick worked pretty well for this guy Archie."

Hoby looked it over. "We'd need oil, a bucket, and a rope," he said. "I think we have all those."

Hoby went down to the garage and found motor oil. The bucket was in the kitchen, and there was a rope in his father's workshop.

"Okay," Zirc said when Hoby came back. "I'll set up the trap while you take him the answer sheet and get the battery. Make sure you come in through the garage and lock the door behind you."

Hoby called Hammerhead.

"Did you get what I wanted, wimp?" Hammerhead asked.

"Y-yeah. I'll give it to you when I get the battery. Meet me at the fence."

Hoby waited at the fence. In a minute Hammerhead lumbered out of his house. Hoby could see he had the battery in his hand.

"Lemme see the answer sheet," Hammerhead demanded.

He grabbed Hoby's arm and took the paper from him. He looked it over, and then laughed softly.

"Nice try, wimp. You think I don't know what math I'm taking?" He crumpled up the paper and threw it at Hoby. "You'll get your battery when I get my answers. Maybe."

Hoby sat down on the grass by the fence. Now what? What was he going to tell Zirc? Why hadn't he stood up to Hammerhead and grabbed that battery? Taz licked his face. "I'm pathetic, boy. Hammerhead's right. I am a wimp."

He left Taz outside and went in through the garage as Zirc had told him.

Up in Hoby's room, Zirc said, "Well, where's the battery? We've got to put it in the freezer."

"Um," Hoby began, but before he could explain there was a scream from the backyard.

Hoby looked out the window and saw his mother's boss, Mr. Vorstenner, spread-eagle on the back steps. Suddenly a torrent of water cascaded past the window and drenched him.

Hoby dashed outside. "Mr. Vorstenner, are you okay?"

Mr. Vorstenner looked around with a dazed expression.

"My. I seem to be quite wet. I must have fallen in a very large puddle. I didn't realize it had rained so much recently."

"Oh yes," Hoby babbled. "We've had lots of rain. Lots and lots of rain. Haven't we, Taz?"

"Yeah a yeah a yeah," said Taz.

"You gotta watch out for those puddles, Mr. Vorstenner," Hoby said, helping him to his feet. "Would you like a towel or something?"

"No thank you, my boy. I think I'd just like to get home. Give these to your mother, please." He handed Hoby a sodden mass of papers and stumbled out the gate to his car.

"Zirc!" Hoby screamed, racing back up the steps to his room.

"Oops," said Zirc. "That was supposed to get Hammerhead, not that other guy."

"Yeah, I know," Hoby said.

"So anyway, did you put the battery in the freezer?" Zirc asked.

"Um, not exactly," Hoby admitted.

"Not exactly? It's not in the freezer?"

"Exactly."

"So where is it?" Zirc asked.

"I'm not exactly sure."

"Hoby. Didn't you get it back from Hammerhead?"

Hoby shook his head. "He knew right away it was the wrong answer sheet. You should have come with me instead of building that dumb trap. Two of us might have been able to do something. I tried, didn't I, Tazzy?"

"Yeah a yeah a yeah," Taz said.

"Veeb. Now what?" Zirc asked.

"Don't worry. We'll think of something," Hoby said. "Won't we, Taz?"

But Taz just let out a long, tired sigh.

Even Taz is losing faith in me, Hoby thought sadly.

chapter thirteen

Hoby stared out the window at the bleak view of Hammerhead's house. The house filled the window, dark and menacing. Hoby pulled down the shade and then flopped down on his bed. He stroked the soft wrinkles in Taz's forehead.

"Your parents must be really worried about you," he said to Zirc.

"Well, I'm hoping they still don't know. See, my grandmother is staying at our house with my little sister, and they think I'm staying at my friend Micon's house. My parents are away until tomorrow. But, tomorrow is my little sister's birthday. I've got to be there."

"My mom is having a baby in a few weeks,"

Hoby told him. "I feel sorry for the poor kid, having a wimp like me for a big brother."

"You're not a wimp. It's just that everyone's a wimp compared to Hammerhead," Zirc told him.

"Patrick and Patience aren't scared of him," Hoby said.

"They don't live next-door to him."

"I wish I could stand up to him. Just once," Hoby said.

"You will, when it really counts," Zirc said.

Hoby hoped Zirc was right. Just then his mother called him for dinner. "I gotta go," he told Zirc. "I'll bring you some food as soon as we're done."

As Hoby sat down at his place at the table, his mom said to his dad, "You know, Mr. Vorstenner is awfully nice, but he can be very odd sometimes."

"Really?" Hoby's dad said.

"Yes," his mom went on. "Today, for example, he brought over some information about the Helman project, and the entire report was soaking wet. I called him to find out what had happened, and he said something about having fallen in a puddle. Then he said what a shame it was that we've had so much rain on our side of town."

"But it hasn't rained in weeks," Hoby's dad said.

Hoby's mom shrugged and shook her head. "He really is a very strange man."

Dinner was pork chops with applesauce, Hoby's favorite.

"You look kind of tired, Hobe. Rough day?" his father asked.

Hoby shrugged. "It was okay. I just didn't sleep too well last night."

"Well, try to get plenty of sleep tonight," his mother said. "There are more pork chops if any-one wants some."

There was a noise from the kitchen. Hoby's mother looked up, puzzled. "Is Tazzy out in the kitchen?" she asked.

"Taz is in his usual spot under Hoby's chair," said his father.

Hoby grabbed his plate and jumped up from the table. "I think I will get some more, Mom." He hurried out to the kitchen.

"Zirc? Is that you?" he whispered.

"Yeah. I was starved. I couldn't wait. I had to eat."

"Quiet. Here comes Mom," Hoby whispered.

The pork chops were gone, and so were most of the vegetables.

Hoby's mother came out and saw the empty dishes. "Well, my goodness. What happened to the rest of the chops?"

"I, kind of, ate them," Hoby said.

"Hoby, you couldn't possibly have eaten two chops and half a bowl of vegetables in the minute you've been out here."

"Yeah, I was really hungry. I just wolfed them down."

His mother looked at him strangely. "You have been eating an awful lot lately. It seems the minute I get back from the grocery store, all the food is gone."

"I think it's a growth spurt, Mom."

"Yes." His mother nodded. "That must be it. I guess I'll just have to start making more food. Well, it'll be good practice for when the baby comes and we have an extra mouth to feed."

"I thought babies only drank milk. He won't be eating pork chops, will he, Mom?"

"Not right away, Hoby, but you'll be amazed at how fast they grow. It won't be long till he or she will be sitting up in the high chair, flinging food all over the place," his mother said happily.

"Great. Something to look forward to," Hoby said.

His mother laughed. "Oh, Hoby, you'll see. It'll be fun. And you'll be a wonderful big brother."

Yeah, the wimp of the world, Hoby thought.

He helped his mother carry out slices of cherry pie for dessert and had just sat back down at the table when the phone rang. Hoby's father answered it.

"No, I'm sorry, there's no one by that name here. You must have the wrong number."

His father put down the phone, smiling. "It sounded like a young lady, looking for someone named Kirk or Dirk, something like that."

Hoby choked on his pie and was still coughing when the phone rang again. He tried to get to it but his father picked it up.

"I'm sorry, young lady, you've reached the same number again, and there's no one named Zirc here.

"Yes. Yes, this is the Hobsons'." The smile vanished from his father's face and he gave Hoby a puzzled look while he spoke into the phone. "You're looking for Hoby's cousin Zirc from Ohio? I see. You met him in school today? I'll tell you what, Sarah Louise, I'll have Hoby call you after he's finished dinner. Perhaps he'll know where to find Cousin Zirc."

Hoby's father hung up the phone. "Apparently we have a new nephew named Zirc. From Ohio."

"How interesting. Would this be my brother's child or your sister's child?" Hoby's mother asked.

"Perhaps we should ask Hoby. He seems to know all about him."

Hoby let out his breath in a loud sigh. "It's a long story. Just a joke, really. I'm not sure you want to hear it."

"I can't speak for Dad, but I'm kind of in the mood for a story. And there's nothing I love better than a good joke," Hoby's mother said.

"Me too," his father said heartily.

Hoby really didn't want to lie to his parents, but he couldn't tell them the truth. He decided to tell them part of the truth. "Well, Zirc is this guy who just moved here, and there's this girl who likes him."

"That would be the girl on the phone?"

"Right. Sarah Louise. And see, this guy Zirc doesn't want anyone to know who he really is, so he sort of made up this story that he's my cousin."

"From Ohio."

"Right."

"He certainly has an unusual name," Hoby's mom said.

"It's Belgian, I think," Hoby told her.

"So Sarah Louise is under the impression that Zirc is staying with you?"

"I guess she is," Hoby said.

"I guess you'd better call her and explain that Zirc doesn't live here anymore."

Before Hoby could answer, the phone rang again. His father picked it up.

"Yes, he's right here. Who shall I say is calling? Carrie? All right, Carrie, just a minute, please."

Hoby felt the blood draining from his face and the strange sound of wind whistling in his head. He looked at the phone his father held out as if it were a gun. "She sounds very anxious to talk to you," his father told him.

Hoby took the phone and walked into the kitchen. "Hello?"

"Hoby?"

"Yeah."

"This is Carrie. Carrie Bateman?"

"Yeah, I figured that. I don't know any other Carries."

"Oh, well, good. I, um, I just wondered if you and Zirc wanted to have lunch with Sarah Louise and me tomorrow."

"Uh, lunch?" Hoby said.

"Yes. You know. In the cafeteria?"

"Yes. I know what lunch is, but um, I don't think I can make it."

"Oh. You won't be in school tomorrow?"

"No, I'll be there, but I have a meeting during lunch. A really important meeting. I couldn't possibly miss it."

"Oh," Carrie said, sounding disappointed. "Well, maybe Friday then. Bye, Hoby."

Hoby hung up the phone. His life had suddenly become very complicated.

chapter fourteen

Between Zirc, Hammerhead, and the new baby, Hoby had a lot on his mind. Too much, in fact. The last thing he needed right now was romance. It wasn't that he disliked Carrie. Carrie was okay. It just wasn't the right time. Hoby knew he wouldn't be able to explain this to Carrie, and he didn't want to hurt her feelings. He decided that the best thing to do was to avoid her. Unfortunately, avoiding Carrie wasn't easy.

The next day at school, Hoby almost ran into her just before morning recess. Luckily, he saw her before she saw him. She was coming down the hall, heading directly toward him. Hoby chose the only possible option and ducked into the janitor's closet.

In the closet he leaned against the wall and waited until he was sure Carrie was gone. He took some deep breaths, grateful for the cool, dark quiet. He was just about to venture out when the door opened.

"Now, where is that light switch?" Hoby heard a familiar voice mumble, and then the light came on.

"Hi, Ms. Tinsley," Hoby said.

"Eeek!" Ms. Tinsley gave a little shriek. "Oh, my goodness, Hoby, you scared me half to death. I didn't expect anyone to be in here."

"Sorry. I didn't mean to scare you," Hoby said.

"I'm looking for a broom," Ms. Tinsley explained. "Someone spilled pencil shavings all over the hall outside my office. I couldn't find Mr. Pinkus, so I decided I'd just get the broom and sweep it up myself. Here we are." She took a broom and dustpan from the rack. She looked carefully at Hoby. "Have you been in here long, Hoby?"

"No. Not too long," Hoby said.

"Mmm-hmm. And what are you doing in here, Hoby, if you don't mind my asking?"

"I was, well, I was hiding," Hoby said.

"Hiding. I see. Were you hiding from anyone in particular, Hoby?"

Hoby didn't want to tell her that he'd been hiding from Carrie. He didn't think she'd understand. So he said, "No. No one in particular. Just hiding."

"Oh my." Ms. Tinsley paused and then went on. "Hoby, dear, I understand that your mother is expecting a new baby. Quite soon, I think, am I right?"

"Yes. It's due in just a few weeks," he said.

"Well, the advent of a new baby can be a very stressful time in the life of a family. Would you say you've been feeling undue stress lately, Hoby?"

"Yeah, maybe. There's kind of a lot going on in my life right now." There was a pause. Ms. Tinsley continued to look at him. Finally Hoby said, "I guess I am kind of worried about what kind of big brother I'll be."

Ms. Tinsley nodded. "Of course you're worried. Being a big brother is an important job."

Hoby had the feeling she was going to say something more on the subject, but the bell rang. "Well," she said brightly, "I'm certainly glad we've had this little talk. Next time you feel like hiding, Hoby, you could try my office. It might be more comfortable than the broom closet. Just come right in and sit down. You won't bother me a bit."

"I'll remember that, Ms. Tinsley," Hoby said.

"All right then. Good-bye, Hoby. Don't forget to turn off the light when you leave."

The next time Hoby almost ran into Carrie was at lunch. He had brought his own sandwich from home, knowing he had to avoid the cafeteria. It was a sunny day, not too cold, so Hoby talked Patrick and Patience into eating outside at the picnic tables. He had just taken a bite of his sandwich when he saw Carrie heading toward his table with her tray. "Yikes," he said. He stuffed the rest of the sandwich into his mouth and jumped over the little wall that divided the picnic area from the playground. All he had to do was crawl along the outside of the wall until he came to the door that led inside. He was almost to the door when he ran headfirst into a pair of legs.

"Hoby? Is that you?"

"Yes, it's me, Ms. Tinsley," Hoby said.

"Have you lost something, Hoby?"

"No, Ms. Tinsley."

"But you were crawling, Hoby."

"Yes. I just felt like crawling."

"Mmm-hmmm. Babies crawl, don't they, Hoby?"

"I guess they do, Ms. Tinsley."

"Maybe you were thinking about that new baby. Do you think that's it, Hoby?"

"I don't really—"

"Just remember, Hoby. It's very normal to have many conflicting feelings about the baby. Whatever you're feeling is okay."

"Right. I'll remember that, Ms. Tinsley."

When he thought about it later, Hoby really couldn't blame Ms. Tinsley for thinking he was acting kind of strange.

chapter
fifteen

When school was finally over, Hoby raced home. In the front yard he saw an old tarp attached to a rope and hanging from a tree. The other end of the rope was tied to the balcony on his house. He found Zirc upstairs.

"What's going on? What's that stuff in the yard?"

"You'll see. It's part of my foolproof plan. All you have to do is call Hammerhead and tell him you've got the copy of the answer sheet. The right one this time."

"But I don't," Hoby said.

"I know. That's okay. Just tell him to come to the front door and you'll give it to him."

Hoby called. "Harold?"

"Whadda you want, wimp?" Hammerhead's voice came spitting out.

"Come on over. We've got the answer sheet. Just come to the front door. I'll wait for you there."

"It better be the right one this time, 'cause if this is another trick, you know what?"

"No, what?" Hoby asked. As soon as he said it he knew it was a mistake. He held the receiver out to Zirc. "I don't think I want to hear this."

Zirc took the receiver and listened. When he hung up, Hoby asked, "So? What'd he say?"

"The usual."

"Bread dough? Apple pie? Peanut butter?"

"Orange juice. Apparently it involves squeezing, mashing, straining the pulp—"

"Enough. I get the picture. Now what?" Hoby asked.

"Everything is taken care of. Now all we have to do is wait."

"Wait for what?" Hoby asked.

There was a muffled scream from the front porch.

"Aha! Our plan goes into action," Zirc said. "Hammerhead has just fallen into our trap."

"Really? Was that him screaming?" Hoby asked.

"Come and look." Zirc led Hoby out onto the little balcony. Below, he could see a struggling mound covered by the tarp. Zirc untied the rope and pulled. The tarp became a tight bundle and slowly rose into the air, where it hung suspended a few inches off the porch.

"Hammerhead is going to be tied up for a while, Hobe," Zirc said happily. "I spent all day making this trap, and believe me, it's a good one." Then he dematerialized. "You stay here and guard him while I go over to his house and get my battery out of the freezer."

Hoby was admiring the trap when Taz started barking on the other side of the house. It wasn't his normal, friendly bark, but a scared, almost desperate bark. Hoby raced downstairs and through the kitchen. Taz stood at the back door.

"What's going on, boy?" Hoby asked. He peered through the kitchen window. "Oh, it's Hammerhead. No wonder Taz is—" A tidal wave of panic washed over him. It couldn't be Hammerhead! Hoby looked again. It was Hammerhead.

But if Hammerhead was at the back door, then who was in the trap?

The phone rang and Hoby grabbed it.

"Hoby?" It was his mom.

"Yes, Mom?"

"I'm going to be home in a few minutes. I just got a most upsetting call from Ms. Tinsley. She sounds very concerned about you. She says you've been talking to yourself and hiding in closets and crawling around on your hands and knees. She said she's going to stop by the house to talk with me."

Hoby's hand on the receiver grew clammy, and wind whistled in his head. A cold wind, colder than any wind he had ever felt. "M-Ms. Tinsley? Would that be the Ms. Tinsley who's my school guidance counselor?"

"Hoby! Has Ms. Tinsley gotten there yet?"

"Actually, there's someone here now," he told her. "I better go. Bye, Mom."

He didn't think his mother needed to know that Ms. Tinsley was wrapped in a tarp and hanging from the front porch.

chapter sixteen

As Hoby hung up the phone he saw Hammer-head coming across the front lawn. He was carrying Zirc's battery in one hand. Hammerhead marched up to the tarp and said, "So, there you are, Hobson, you little creep. I guess you got caught in your own trap, huh? I knew this was a trick. I knew you wouldn't get that answer sheet like you promised, and now I'm going to flunk my math test without those answers. I should have known better than to think you could steal anything. And if you think your friend is going to get his battery back, you're dumber than I thought. You know what I'm going to do to you?" Hammerhead took hold of the rope and began swinging it.

Hoby rushed outside. "Don't worry, Ms. Tinsley, I'll get you out of there."

There was a muffled moan from the tarp. Hoby ran full speed into Hammerhead and knocked him out of the way. The battery flew out of Hammerhead's hand, and Hoby dove to get it. Then, before Hammerhead could retaliate, Hoby tackled him.

When Hammerhead was flat on his back, Hoby ran to the tarp. "I'm coming, Ms. Tinsley. Hang on." Suddenly the bundle began to lower itself onto the sidewalk. Hoby looked up and saw the rope untying itself. Zirc, he thought. Hammerhead picked himself up and headed for Hoby like a charging bull. Hoby danced out of his way just in time. Hammerhead spun around and started for Hoby again, but this time a rope wrapped itself around Hammerhead's legs, and he fell flat on his face. In the next second Hoby had the tarp open. "Are you okay, Ms. Tinsley?"

"Oh my," Ms. Tinsley muttered. "My goodness."

Hoby helped her get to her feet. "You're not hurt, are you, Ms. Tinsley?"

"No, dear. I'm quite all right. Just a bit shaken up." Hoby held her arm while she dusted herself off. "Thank you, Hoby."

"I think Harold thought I was the one in the trap," Hoby said.

"Yes, he did. No doubt he was planning to torment you. No wonder you've been acting peculiarly lately. Anyone would under that kind of stress." She looked at Hammerhead, whose arms and legs were now securely tied. "And as for you, Mr. Jones. You are a bully and a cheat. I shall see to it that you are dealt with accordingly."

Hammerhead moaned. He looked dazed. Just then a car pulled into the driveway. Hoby's mom hopped out and came toward them. "Ms. Tinsley," she said. "I'm so sorry I'm late. Please forgive me, and please explain to me what this is all about. I must agree that Hoby has been behaving strangely lately, but I think it's just anxiety about the baby. Hoby tends to be a worrier."

"Mrs. Hobson, I understand everything now. This big bully here has been threatening him," Ms. Tinsley said, nodding at Hammerhead. "Why, he even had a trap laid out for Hoby." Ms. Tinsley smiled bravely. "But I'm afraid he caught more than he bargained for this time. As you see, Hoby has managed to subdue him."

"Hoby subdued a bully?" Hoby's mother looked very surprised.

"Yes, and Hoby freed me from this trap single-handedly. Why, he practically saved my life," Ms. Tinsley went on.

"Hoby saved your life?" his mother said.

"He's a very good boy, Mrs. Hobson."

"Yes. Yes, he is." Hoby's mother sounded pleased but slightly dazed.

Ms. Tinsley marched over to Hammerhead, grabbed the rope around his hands, and yanked him to his feet. "Come along, Harold. I think your mother will be very interested in what I have to tell her."

"Hoby, let's go inside. I want to hear all about this," his mom said.

"I'll be right there, Mom."

As soon as his mom went in, Hoby said, "Zirc? Where are you?"

"Right here." With a zap he materialized. "I guess we fixed Hammerhead, huh?"

"I'll say. Here's your battery." Hoby handed it to him.

Zirc took the battery and clasped it to his chest. "I've never been so happy to see anything in my entire life. Now I can finally get home! Come on. Come with me to the space cruiser."

"I have to go inside and talk to my mom for a

minute. You go on ahead. I'll be right there."

"Okay. But hurry."

Hoby went inside.

"Hoby," his mom called from the kitchen. "I think this calls for a celebration." His mom was going through her file of recipes. "Here it is. Aunt Jesse's Double Chocolate Cake with Triple Fudge Frosting."

"Mom? What about the pact? What about the baby? What about chocolate being bad for you?"

"Oh, Hoby, quit being such a worrier. It's not every day that my son gets the best of a big bully like Harold Jones and saves his school counselor's life! I don't know what happened out there, but whatever it was, Ms. Tinsley went from thinking you were, in her words, 'exhibiting problem behavior' to thinking you're wonderful. However you managed it, I think we should celebrate. Come on. Help me make this cake."

His mother took a bowl out of the cabinet and read the recipe. "Okay, let's see, we need—Yikes!"

She was staring straight ahead, her hand on her stomach, her eyes huge.

"Mom? What?"

"It's nothing, Hoby. I think I just need to sit down for a—Yikes!"

"Mom?"

"Well, maybe it's something," she said, easing herself into a chair. "There. That's better. I think it's just—Yikes!"

"Mom?"

"It's definitely something, Hoby. You better call your father. Tell him to come home right away."

Hoby ran to the phone and called his father at the office.

"Dad? Mom said to call you. She said you should come home right away."

"Is this it, Hoby? Is the baby coming?"

"I don't know, Dad. Mom keeps saying yikes!"

"Uh-oh, that's what she said when you came. How often is she saying yikes, Hoby?"

"About every three minutes," Hoby said.

"Yikes," said his father. "Call your grandmother. Call Mrs. Bidwell. Call Dr. Jamison. I'll be right home, Hoby. Just stay with your mother until I get there."

Hoby hung up and ran back to his mom. "You okay, Mom? You want anything? A glass of water? A wet towel? Chocolate?"

"Do you have any chocolate, Hoby?"

"No, but I could start making that cake."

"We'll make it later. Right now we have to make some phone calls. Yikes!"

Hoby stayed with his mother while she made the calls. Finally, she put the phone down and said, "Well, Dr. Jamison will meet us at the hospital, so as soon as your father gets home we'll go. Gram is on her way over to stay with you, Hoby. Yikes!

"Did you want a boy or a girl, Hoby?"

"Either," he said. "I just want you and the baby to be okay."

"Oh, Hoby, thank you." She put her arms around him and hugged him. "Yikes," she said.

It was only fifteen minutes until his father got there, but it seemed like the longest fifteen minutes of Hoby's life. By the time he came, the yikeses were only two minutes apart.

Hoby's grandmother got there just as his parents were leaving.

"We'll call you as soon as we know anything," his father said.

"Yikes!" said his mom.

chapter seventeen

Hoby's grandmother said, "Well, we might have a long wait ahead of us. I suggest Monopoly." She sat down at the kitchen table. Hoby was looking for the Monopoly game when Taz trotted over and dropped a green jumpsuit at his feet.

"Oh, my gosh—Zirc. He's still waiting," Hoby cried. He had told Zirc he would be right there. How long ago was that? Almost two hours ago. "I gotta go, Gram. A friend of mine left this here and I've got to get it back. I'll play Monopoly when I come back."

"All right, Hoby. Don't be long," she said.

"Come on, Tazzy." Hoby grabbed the green jumpsuit and raced out the door.

Patrick and Patience came through the gate as Hoby and Taz barreled down the steps.

"Hoby! What happened? We heard you beat up Hammerhead and saved Ms. Tinsley's life!" Patrick said.

"You're a hero, Hobe," Patience told him.

"It wasn't anything, really. And I did have some help," Hoby said modestly.

"That's not what we heard. We heard you did it single-handedly."

"I'll explain it all later. Right now I've got to hurry. I've got to return this to someone before he leaves."

"Can we come with you?" Patience asked.

"Sure. But we have to hurry. He's been waiting almost two hours."

They would finally get to meet Zirc. Hoby led them through the woods to the place where the space cruiser had been. At least where he thought it had been.

"Wait. Maybe it was over this way more," he said, plowing farther into the woods.

"What are we looking for, Hobe?"

"A space cruiser," Hoby told them.

"A what?"

"A space cr—oh, never mind." There was no sign of Zirc or of the space cruiser.

He led them back to the original spot, the place he was sure it had been parked.

"This is the right place, isn't it, Tazzy?"

Taz sniffed at the ground and said, "Yeah a yeah a yeah."

There were marks on the ground where the wheels had been.

"I guess we're too late. I never even got to say good-bye," Hoby said sadly.

"Say good-bye to who?"

"To Zi—" Hoby stopped. Zirc was gone. Patrick and Patience would never believe him now. There was no point in trying to get them to. "Never mind. Look, I gotta get home. My mom's about to have her baby, and my grandmother's waiting for me to play Monopoly. Want to play?"

"Sure," said Patrick, and the three of them went back to Hoby's.

chapter eighteen

Hoby sat on the couch, holding his new baby brother. Thomas had miniature hands and feet, a tiny mouth that moved constantly, and deep blue eyes that seemed to know a lot of things already, even though he was only three days old.

But he was so tiny, so fragile. He had such a long way to go before he was grown up and old enough to take care of himself. There were a lot of things that could go wrong with a baby.

"What's that red blotch on his forehead, Mom? Is that normal?" Hoby asked.

"Yes, Hoby. All babies have blotches," his mom said.

"He's making a strange face, Mom, like he's in pain or something. Is that normal?"

"Yes, Hoby, all babies make strange faces." She came over to the couch and looked at him. "I think maybe he's ready for a nap. Shall we put him in his crib? Then we can make that chocolate cake while he's sleeping."

Hoby handed Thomas to his mother. She took him into the nursery, changed his diaper, and put him in his crib. They watched him as he squirmed himself into a comfortable position. Taz peered through the bars of the crib, watching the baby, too.

"Do you ever wonder what he'll be like when he grows up?" Hoby asked.

"Of course I do. But I'm pretty confident that he'll be wonderful," his mom said.

"You are? How do you know?" Hoby asked.

His mother put an arm around Hoby and gave him a squeeze. "Well, look at what a wonderful big brother he has. How can he miss? Right, Tazzy?"

"Yeah a yeah a yeah," said Taz.

While the baby slept, Hoby and his mom made the chocolate cake and then put it in the oven.

"It still has to bake for another half hour," his mom said. "Why don't you take Taz out for a walk, and by the time you come back it'll be done."

"Okay," Hoby said. Now that Hammerhead was grounded Hoby could go outside without worrying about being pounded. It was a good feeling. He wasn't scared of him anymore.

Hoby followed Taz through the woods, not really paying much attention to where they were going. He was thinking about earlier that day. Carrie had sat down beside him at the lunch table. At first he had been almost too nervous to eat. But when Carrie gave him one of the chocolate fudge brownies that she had gotten for dessert, Hoby decided that he didn't mind sitting with Carrie. He actually kind of liked it. He was wondering if she would sit with him again tomorrow when he heard Taz barking.

Taz was standing a few feet in front of Hoby, looking at a tree.

"What's going on, Tazzy?" Hoby asked.

He drew closer. That's when he saw it. Pinned to the tree with his father's screwdriver was a note.

It was from Zirc!

Dear Hoby,

 The battery works great. The cruiser started right up. I'm scared to turn it off in case something goes wrong, and I think I better get home while I can.

Thanks for everything. I don't know what I would have done without your help. I guess you proved to Hammerhead that you are no wimp. I knew you would stand up to him when it counted.

When I get my cruiser's license my friend Micon and I will come back and see you. Maybe we'll take you to our time for a visit.

You're zall, Hoby.

Your friend,
Zirc

P.S. Say hi to Sarah Louise for me.

Hoby folded the note carefully and put it in his pocket. "He'll be back someday, boy," Hoby told him.

"Yeah a yeah a yeah," said Taz.

Time Traveler's Dictionary

atmos-stasis *(n)* A system that regulates weather over urban or heavily populated areas.

dematerializer *(n)* A device worn on the wrist that, when activated, enables one to become invisible through molecular redistribution. Dematerializers are available for pets as well, but these are worn on the collar rather than the wrist and are activated only by the pet's owner.

flibbin' *(adj) Slang.* Extremely annoying or irritating. [Usage: "My flibbin' parents won't let me go out until I've cleaned up my room."]

flizball *(n)* A sport played in a three-dimensional, gravity-controlled court with a soft ball five inches in diameter. The ball may be kicked or hit with a fliz mallet. The game is won by the team with the most goals scored after two twenty-minute periods. Goals are scored by inserting the ball into one of ten fliz catchers that are distributed throughout the court.

greeb *(adj) Slang.* Extremely dirty and odorous; badly in need of a wash. [Usage: "Your sneakers are really greeb."]

IPS [*In*ter*p*lanetary *S*trife] *(n)* Disagreement and fighting between planetary colonies.

knap [*Kn*owledge *ap*praisal] *(n)* Method of testing or ascertaining how much knowledge a student has absorbed. Knaps are administered by means of a device known as a knapler.

knapler *(n)* Apparatus that measures a student's knowledge. Each student is fitted with a custom-designed headset that reads brain waves to measure cognitive understanding.

mord [*M*olecular *R*estructuring *D*evice] *(n)* A device that repairs broken objects by restructuring the molecules.

phero-atomizing fluid *(n)* Fluid that, when sprayed, causes a molecular reaction that creates a temporary force field barrier.

razzed up *(adj)* Not functioning properly; confused; in disarray. [Usage: "Hammerhead Jones is one razzed up human being."]

robo-cleaner *(n)* A specially programmed appliance that cleans, straightens, and restores order to rooms. Each room may have its own robo-cleaner, but some houses are equipped with central-robo, which cleans each room simultaneously.

soundport *(n)* Audio system found in most space

cruisers. Modern soundports offer a database of over one million pieces of music.

tempulator *(n)* An appliance used to keep food at the most appropriate temperature. Most tempulators allow for twenty different settings simultaneously.

time module *(n)* Apparatus found on many space cruisers that enables the cruiser to navigate through time. When the time module is activated, the cruiser remains stationary in space but moves through time. Children under eighteen are prohibited from time traveling unless accompanied by an adult.

veeb *(interj) Slang.* Indicating a bad or perilous situation. [Usage: "Veeb! I forgot my math homework for the third day in a row."]

yadzuu *(n) Slang.* A clumsy person—one who trips, drops things, and spills frequently. [Usage: "I'd let you hold the baby if you weren't such a yadzuu."]

zall *(interj) Slang.* Cool; excellent; awesome. [Usage: "This new video game is really zall."]